THE CROW WHO CAME TO STAY

written and illustrated by

JUDY VARGA

William Morrow and Company
New York 1967

A crow named Clyde was flying high in the sky,
looking for a meal and a place to rest,
when his sharp eyes noticed something black and shiny below.
Always curious, he decided to find out what it was.

When he got closer,
Clyde saw that it was a shiny black top hat
on the head of a scarecrow in a corn patch.
Clyde liked the scarecrow at once,
because of his jolly, smiling face,
so he decided to stay awhile.
He hoped that he would find something to eat nearby,
but all he could see was corn, and he did not like corn.
Other crows did, but not he.
Suddenly Clyde smelled something he did like—
freshly baked cherry pie.
It was cooling on a windowsill.

Clyde looked around; there was no one to see.
So he feasted, first picking out the juicy cherries,
then going to work on the delicious piecrust.
He was almost finished when an angry man chased him away.

Clyde settled back on the friendly scarecrow's hat, sighing.
He was used to being chased, for nobody seemed to like a crow.
Soon he saw the man and his wife rushing toward him.
The man shook his fists and shouted, "Shoooo!

You ate my dessert, you nasty crow.
And, in case you don't know,
that scarecrow is there to scare crows away.
You're not supposed to sit on its head.
Shoooo! Go away, crow!"

But Clyde did not move; he liked to be near the scarecrow.
He had heard that "Shoooo! Go away, crow!"
so many times before
that by now he could say the words quite clearly himself.
Sometimes people got tired of chasing him and left him alone,
but this man pulled off his boots and hurled one at Clyde.
So Clyde decided to move,
and he flew to the lowest branch of the apple tree.
The man would have thrown the other boot at him as well
if his wife had not grabbed it away from him, saying,
"I'm ashamed of you, Mr. Pepperpot!"
Mr. Pepperpot put his boots back on
and gave Clyde a nasty look.
"I'm going inside now for my supper," he said.
"Don't let me find you around when I come out in the morning."

But as soon as Mr. and Mrs. Pepperpot went inside,
Clyde settled back on the scarecrow.
He did not want to leave
the friendly face of the scarecrow ever again.
When it began to rain,
Clyde snuggled under the scarecrow's coat.
It was cozy, warm, and dry in there.

Clyde slept until the sun came up.
Then he woke, because he smelled bacon frying.
He stole some bacon and was very surprised
when Mrs. Pepperpot smiled,
every bit as prettily as the scarecrow,
and put more bacon on the windowsill
and a piece of cherry pie too.

When he was full, Clyde walked into the kitchen to look around.
Then Mr. Pepperpot came into the kitchen and saw the crow.
He shooed and shouted and frightened Clyde so much
that Clyde began to squawk as loud as he could.
"I will not have that crow around," yelled Mr. Pepperpot.
"The first ears of corn are almost ripe.
This pesty crow will call in every other crow
from all over the countryside with his squawking.
Then there will not be a single ear of corn left for us."
Mr. Pepperpot threw an apron over Clyde
and grabbed him so tightly
that most of Clyde's feathers got ruffled.
"I think I'll take care of him right now," said Mr. Pepperpot.
Mrs. Pepperpot screamed and helped Clyde get free.
"I will not have you bully that poor crow," she said.
"He hasn't done anything bad yet,
and he can stay until he does."

Clyde fled to the top of the cupboard,
cackling and whistling and flapping his wings angrily.
Mr. Pepperpot left the house in a huff, without his breakfast,
and stood guarding his corn patch all morning.
Clyde finished off Mr. Pepperpot's breakfast
and stayed in the kitchen to play with Mrs. Pepperpot.
He came every morning after that,
because they had such a good time together.
But as soon as Mr. Pepperpot came in from the corn patch,
Clyde left. He hated to be shouted at.

Whenever Mr. Pepperpot was in the house,
Clyde went to visit his friend the scarecrow.
Every night he slept on the scarecrow's fine tall hat.
He knew that the scarecrow was glad to see him.
Why else would he smile whenever they were together?

Eating lunch one day, with a long frown on his face,
Mr. Pepperpot glared at Clyde,
who was perched on the scarecrow's hat
catching bugs that flew by.
He did not want the crow to do him any favors,
since he had made up his mind
to get rid of him once and for all,
before something happened to his precious corn patch.
After lunch Mrs. Pepperpot went upstairs to nap.

As soon as she was out of sight,
Mr. Pepperpot sneaked up on Clyde,
a shovel raised high.

Just as he lowered it, Clyde swooped forward
to gobble up a beetle that had tried to avoid him.
Crash! went the shovel, crushing the scarecrow's fine hat.
Rip! went the scarecrow's cotton face as it tore in two.
Zoom! flew Clyde to his friend's aid,
screaming and pecking at Mr. Pepperpot's shiny bald head.

Mrs. Pepperpot came rushing outside.
"I saw it all," she said,
"and I must say that you deserve everything you got.
Whatever is wrong with you, Mr. Pepperpot?
You used to be a kindly man."
Mr. Pepperpot ran into the house
to put a cold compress on his aching head.
Clyde cuddled close to the scarecrow,
cackling and cawing to him softly.
Instead of a smile, the scarecrow now wore a sad frown
and would not cheer up no matter what Clyde did.

Cawing sadly to the sick scarecrow,
Clyde decided he would leave
but not until his friend began to smile again.
Even though it did not rain that night
Clyde snuggled under the scarecrow's coat.
He was sure that his friend wanted him as close as possible.
When Mrs. Pepperpot brought out
a steaming plate of hamburgers for his supper,
Clyde did not move.
Although she called and called to him,
he stayed where he was.
Never before had Clyde felt so sad
that he could not eat a meal.

When Mr. Pepperpot woke in the morning
and did not see the crow in his usual perching place
and did not see him in the kitchen eating bacon,
he felt very happy.
Even though his head hurt still,
he whistled a happy little tune as he sat down to eat.
"Some of the corn will be ripe today," he told his wife.
"We can have homegrown corn on the cob for supper."
But Mrs. Pepperpot did not answer.
She missed the crow very much
and did not feel like being friendly.
Besides, from the distance, she could hear a noise that
every farmer hopes he will never hear—
the flapping of hundreds of wings
and the cawing of hundreds of noisy mouths.

Mr. and Mrs. Pepperpot ran outside and watched with horror
as an army of hungry crows landed on the golden ears of corn.
"Your spiteful friend is back, bringing all his relatives,"
shouted Mr. Pepperpot,
looking for something to frighten the crows with.
He began to run to the corn patch,
even though he knew that by the time he got there
most of the damage would be done.

Under the scarecrow's coat
Clyde also heard the arrival of the hungry crows.
He would have liked to chase them,
because he wanted to help his sick friend do his job.
But he realized that he could not fight so many crows
and decided to stay out of sight.
Angrily, he began to scream the words he knew so well,
"Shoooo! Go away, crow!" over and over again.

The crows never had seen a talking scarecrow before.
Frightened, they moved away like a big black cloud
without touching a kernel on a single stalk of corn.
Mr. Pepperpot could not believe his eyes and ears.
Who was doing the shouting?
He knew very well that scarecrows do not talk.
Mr. Pepperpot ran to the scarecrow, his wife behind him.
Clyde tried to hide; his heart beat very fast.
But Mr. Pepperpot probed and poked through the straw.
At last he found Clyde, who tried to fly away.

But Mr. Pepperpot held him fast and said,
"Don't go away, crow! Let's make a fresh start."
Then he bowed politely, saying, "Welcome to our farm."
After Clyde and Mr. Pepperpot had inspected
the rows and rows of golden corn,
Mrs. Pepperpot fetched a needle and thread
and repaired the scarecrow's torn face.
In no time at all he was smiling again
as prettily as Mr. and Mrs. Pepperpot were smiling.
But she left the hat just as it was
to remind Mr. Pepperpot of a sad mistake.

That night Mr. and Mrs. Pepperpot
had homegrown corn on the cob for dinner.
They offered some to Clyde, but he did not like corn.
Instead, he ate two freshly baked cherry pies all by himself.